SHREK 2™
GAG BOOK

By Sarah Fisch
and Howie Dewin

SCHOLASTIC INC.

New York   Toronto   London   Auckland   Sydney
Mexico City   New Delhi   Hong Kong   Buenos Aires

0-439-53848-3

Shrek is a registered trademark of DreamWorks L.L.C.
Shrek 2 TM and © 2004 DreamWorks L.L.C. All rights reserved.

Published by Scholastic Inc.
SCHOLASTIC and associated logos are trademarks and/or registered trademarks of Scholastic Inc.

12 11 10 9 8 7 6 5 4 3 2 1   4 5 6 7 8/0

Printed in the U.S.A.
First printing, May 2004

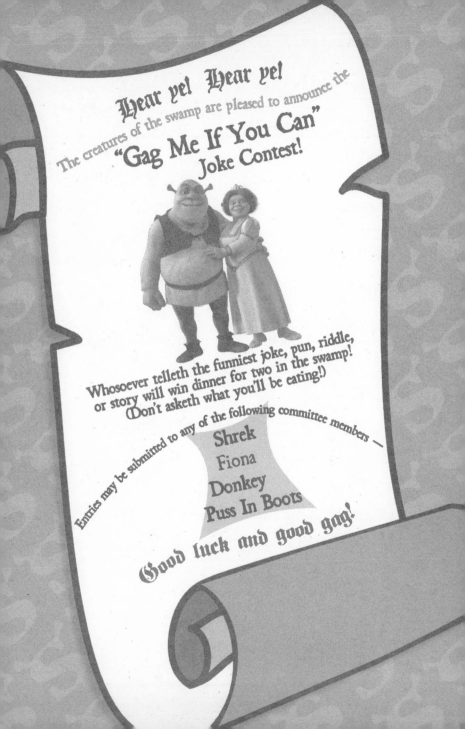

From the Law Offices of the Three Blind Mice
We fight injustice wherever we see it!

What do you call a mouse in a suit of armor?

A no-dent rodent!

Where's the best place for a mouse to leave his boat?

The Hickory Dickory Dock.

What's gray and has big ears and a trunk?

A mouse on vacation.

How many blind mice does it take to change a lightbulb?

Oh, come on! Who needs light?

Are You A Blind Mouse?

IF

YOR

TAILIZ

MISSING

B4UCTHECAT

THEANSWERIZYES

We want you to feel at home!

What vegetable do you get when Shrek runs through your garden?

Squash!

Why did Baby Bear cross the playground?

To get to the other slide.

Does Goldilocks get enough to eat when she has dinner with Mama, Papa, and Baby?

Bearly.

What do you call Baby Bear's great-grandmother and great-grandfather?

The Three Bears' Forebears.

Goldilocks's Guide to Dining Out . . .

If your eggs move fast, they're too runny.

If your hamburger won't put down its book, it's too read.

If your toast asks questions you can't answer, it's too hard.

If your mother tells you to eat your lima beans and you don't want to, it's too bad.

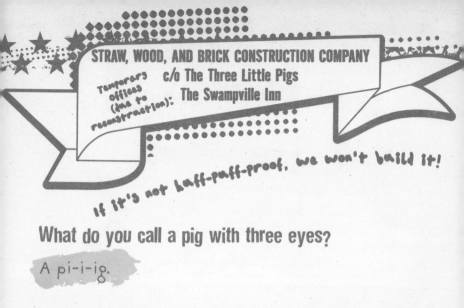

STRAW, WOOD, AND BRICK CONSTRUCTION COMPANY

Temporary offices (due to reconstruction):

c/o The Three Little Pigs

The Swampville Inn

If it's not huff-puff-proof, we won't build it!

What do you call a pig with three eyes?

A pi-i-ig.

What do you get when you cross a pig with a robot?

A cy-pork!

What do you call it when a pig runs away?

A ham scram!

What do you get when you cross Pinocchio with a pig?

Pine swine!

If a red house is made of red bricks, a blue house is made from blue bricks, and a pink house is made from pink bricks — what's a green house made from?

GLASS!

What's the Three Pigs' favorite horror movie?

The Texas Chain-sow Massacre!

What does a pig wear when he gets dressed up?

A pigsty.

What do you use when you arrest a bad pig?

Ham cuffs.

Why do pigs like to spend so much time in the kitchen?

Because we always feel like bacon.

Pinocchio vs. Gingerbread Man

Why does Pinocchio like to float in the ocean?

He wants to be a real buoy!

Why does Pinocchio always stop lying when his nose gets to be eleven inches long?

Because he doesn't want it to turn into a foot!

What do you get when you cross Pinocchio with chocolate custard?

Wooden puddin'!

What do you get when you cross a DJ with the Gingerbread Man?

Sweet beats

How many gingerbread men does it take to change a lightbulb?

Two — one to change the bulb, and the other to scrape the burnt parts off him!

Why was the Gingerbread Man crying?

Because his mom was a wafer so long.

Glass Slipper Inc.

c/o PRINCE CHARMING & CINDERELLA
charming castle, Penthouse
Far Far Away 12000

Let us shatter your notions of footwear.

Why couldn't Prince Charming get down from the tower?

Because he was totally stuck-up.

What do you call Prince Charming after a sword fight with Puss In Boots?

Minced Charming!

How did Shrek feel when he saw Princess Fiona talking to Prince Charming?

He was green with envy!

Why did Cinderella get kicked off the basketball team?

Because she ran away from the ball.

Why was Cinderella such a bad athlete?

Because her coach was a pumpkin!

How many Prince Charmings does it take to change a lightbulb?

One. He just holds it in the air and waits for the world to revolve around him!

Cinderella: Hey, Prince, why did you choose me to be your princess?

Charming: That's easy. You were a shoe in!

SLEEPING BEAUTY
MATTRESS COMPANY

You've never slept like this before!

Why did Puss In Boots ask Sleeping Beauty to help him find new slippers?

He wanted a sleeping bootie.

Why did Sleeping Beauty fall asleep at the photo shop?

She was waiting for her prints to come.

Why weren't the Three Little Pigs invited to the royal ball?

Because they're so boar-ing.

TOP TEN WAYS TO TELL IF YOUR PRINCE IS A FROG:

10. He gets a little too excited when there are flies in the house.

9. He gets jumpy in French restaurants.

8. His best friends live in the pond.

7. It takes a day to get him out of the bath.

6. He thinks he's related to salad, broccoli, lima beans, and anything else that's green.

5. He uses his tongue to do the dusting.

4. He always wins underwater swimming contests.

3. You can't find his toes.

2. Kermit is his favorite actor.

1. There's always a wet mark when he gets off a stool.

He croaked up.

What did the frog do when he heard my jokes?

your wish is our command!

What do you call Puss In Boots when he steals potions from the Fairy Godmother?

A cat burglar!

How many Fairy Godmothers does it take to change a lightbulb?

It depends what you want to change it into. . . .

What did the witch request when she stayed at a hotel?

Broom service.

That Spells Trouble!

Frog Spell + Bunny Spell = A Ribbit

Frog Spell + Eye Doctor Spell = Hoptometrist

Frog Spell + Vegetable Spell = Green Bean

Frog Spell + Hero Spell = Knight in Sliming Armor

Rhyme Time

Make up your own spells.
All you need are a couple of
rhymes for some of the important
ingredients and you'll be making spells
in no time! For example . . .

Newt Eye: Fruit Pie: Mute Guy

Squeeze the juice of a newt eye into a fruit pie
and turn talkers to mute guys.

Frog Gut: Dog Butt: Bog Mutt

One cup of frog gut rubbed on a dog's butt turns
enemies to bog mutts.

Scum Slime: Some Time: Dumb Crime

Boil some scum slime and stir it for some time, and
your rival will be arrested for doing a dumb crime.

Why do so many rabbits play in Rumpelstiltskin's yard when he spins straw into gold?

They heard he was making karats!

What did Rumpelstiltskin say when the reporter asked if he could call him by his first name?

Be my guess.

What did Rumpelstiltskin say when the young girl finally guessed "Rumpelstiltskin"?

That's my gnome!

Rumpelstiltskin's Top Ten Great Names for a Baby

10. Beetsme
9. Guessagain
8. Idunno
7. Gimmeahint
6. Amiright

5. Imstumped
4. Whoknows
3. Noclue
2. Tizzamystery
1. Youllneverguess

What happened when the mama cat ate a ball of wool?

She had mittens!

Who do the three little kittens still believe in?

Santa Claws.

What do kittens get after they've been playing out in the forest?

Fir coats.

What do kittens say when we get a spanking for losing our mittens?

Me-Ow!

More than
3,000,000
mittens lost!

Why are kittens so small?

Because we only drink condensed milk.

Who's the funniest of them all?

SHREK!

What happens when Shrek . . .

. . . falls off a boat?

He goes ogreboard.

. . . eats too much?

He gets ogreweight.

. . . burns his dinner?

The food gets ogredone.

. . . gets too emotional?

He is ogrecome.

. . . has buckteeth?

He's got an ogrebite.

ode to Green

Green is the color of my true love's skin.

It's the sheen on the mold for penicillin.

It's the cast you will see if you witness me grin

and the shade of the boogers I pull from within.

Top Ten Reasons Shrek Is in a Bad Mood

10. His favorite meals have all just been declared endangered species.

9. He fell in the swamp and got a little bogged down.

8. Fiona cleaned the house.

7. He ran out of his favorite cologne, Mold Spice.

6. It's not easy being green.

5. He was playing chess with Fiona, and he got Shrek-mated.

4. The swamp diner stopped serving his favorite breakfast, toe jam and toast.

3. He's got a bad case of swamp gas.

2. Donkey ate all his favorite ice cream flavor, Loogies n' Cream.

And the number one reason Shrek is having a bad day is . . .

1. He took a swim in the swamp and accidentally got clean.

Knock, Knock! GO AWAY!

Knock, knock.

Who's there?

Ogre!

Ogre who?

O-gre take a
flying leap!

Knock, knock.

Who's there?

Ogre!

Ogre who?

Ogre my dead body
will I let you in!

Knock, knock.

Who's there?

Donkey!

Donkey who?

Donk-ey know I don't want any visitors?

Knock, knock.

Who's there?

Dragon

Dragon who?

**Dragon out of here . . .
you're going too slow!**

Knock, knock.

Who's there?

Puss!

Puss who?

**Puss the gate shut
on your way out!**

FIONA'S FAVORITE FUNNIES!

Favorite Place? Shrekoslovakia!

Favorite Singer? Britney Spew

Why did Princess Fiona buy a shovel store?

She wanted to be the Queen of Spades!

Why did Princess Fiona go to medical school?

She wanted to be the Queen of Hearts!

Why did Princess Fiona go out dancing every night?

She wanted to be the Queen of Clubs!

Why did Princess Fiona go to the jewelry store?

To be the Queen of Diamonds, of course!

Through an Ogre's Eyes: How to Stay Beautiful

Hair: Be sure to wash your hair as seldom as possible. Don't risk running out of oil for the bugs and other critters in there.

Skin: Bathe regularly in water that is (at least) as thick as a hearty pea soup.

Teeth: Brush only after you have run out of all possible storage space between your molars.

Fingernails: Keep them long, but beware too sharp a point on the end. Otherwise nose-picking can be hazardous to your health.

Toenails: Don't overindulge. Allow several weeks between harvesting. The longer the jam sits there, the better it will be.

Figure: Don't sweat the big stuff. Consider this:

Once I was a beauty and all I did was preen,

Getting ready for my prince on the
day I would be queen.

Then I met an ogre, the most handsome thing I'd seen

And now I couldn't be happier that
I'm plump and really green.

Disclaimer: Fiona prefers to shower more often,
but sometimes she goes gross to keep her ogre happy.

OGRESS HUMOR

Why did Fiona leave the kingdom of Far Far Away and move to the swamp?

She wanted to live in the shrub-urbs!

How does Fiona keep all her books so well organized?

She's an alphabetical ogre!

What do you get when you cross an ogre with a basketball player?

Shrekille O'Neal!

What do Shrek and Fiona like to do after dinner?

Go out for an evening troll.

What's brown and slimy and squirms when you poke it?

Shrek's dinner!

What did the ogre say to the waiter?

There aren't enough flies in my soup!

Rap It UP!

I'm poppin' like balloons, I'm rockin' like a chair,

I got so much bling they call me the mule-ionnaire!

I'm the slammin' MC from the cool swamp scene,

And I got mad rhymes like Shrek's got green!

He's big as a house, he's mean as a snake,

When it comes to farts and boogers, yo, Shrek really takes the cake!

He's a nasty swamp monster, but I love him to the end,

'Cause that stinky slimy ogre is my very best friend!

once upon a time!!!

Shrek went out to gather firewood. While he was in the forest, he saw Donkey standing in the middle of the swamp, shouting for no reason.

Shrek didn't say anything to Donkey. But the next day, he saw Donkey yelling and shouting in the empty swamp again. And again the next day. Finally, on the fourth day, when Shrek saw Donkey yelling and screaming again, he decided he'd better say something.

"Hey, Donkey," Shrek called. "What are you yelling at?"

Donkey looked at Shrek and said, "Fiona told me if I shouted enough, I'd become **a little horse!**"

A DONKEY'S IDEA OF FUN

What do you call a three-legged donkey?

A wonkey!

Why did the donkey go stand out in the blizzard?

He wanted to be a cool mule!

How do you make a dragonfly?

Take away her skateboard!

What do you call a donkey who does all his chores?

A thorough burro!

Puss's Vocabulary Lesson #1

To be very, very angry	Fur-ious
A luxury automobile	Cat-illac
An ideal situation	Purr-fect
A golfer's assistant	Cat-tie
A slight delay	A paws
Product to improve garden	Fur-talizer

Knock, knock.

Who's there?

Cattle.

Cattle who?

**This cattle drive
you crazy!**

Gotta Fur Ball? Don't Throw It Away!

Puss's Top Ten Ways To Use Those Old Fur Balls:

10. Earrings (clasps sold separately)

9. Buttons (no holes needed)

8. Checkerboard pieces (separate dark from light)

7. Blankets (for those with a large collection)

6. Pot holders (for those with a smaller collection)

5. Cotton balls (allow to dry before using)

4. Trail markers (select thickest ones)

3. Mice repellents (select smelliest ones)

2. Children's toy (excellent for learning to count)

1. Adhesive (use when wet)

PUSS IN BOOTS'S SCHOOL OF COMEDY

What kind of parties does Puss In Boots throw?

Hair balls!

What is Puss In Boots's favorite TV show?

The evening mews!

Why did Puss In Boots get a ticket?

For kitty littering!

Why does Puss In Boots like to listen to other cats howling in the night?

Because it's meow-sic to his ears!

What does Puss In Boots like to put on his hamburger?

Catsup!

Why does Puss In Boots always win at video games?

He gets nine lives!

What do you call Puss In Boots in love?

A smitten kitten!

What would Puss In Boots call the kingdom if he were allowed to rename it?

The kingdom of Fur Fur Away!

What does Puss In Boots grow in his garden?

Cattails and pussy willows!

What does Puss In Boots do when his computer crashes?

He re-boots it!

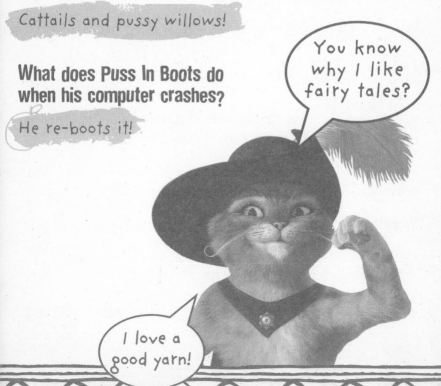

You know why I like fairy tales?

I love a good yarn!

H & G BAKERY AND CAFE
Wicked Witch (a)Way
Far Far Away 54321

FOLLOW THE TRAIL TO THE BEST BAKERY IN TOWN!

What happened when the Wicked Witch fell into the vat of candle wax?

She turned into a wicked wick.

Why did the warlock get confused when his wife gave birth to twins?

He couldn't tell which witch was witch.

Why did the witch give up telling fortunes?

There was no future in it.

Why wouldn't the witch go on vacation?

She was afraid she'd get broom sick.

JACK'S PRUNING
AND
LANDSCAPING
BEANSTALK LANE
FAR FAR UP 99999

No vegetable too tall...

Which vegetable helped me find my missing golden egg?

A potato. It was good at keeping its eyes peeled.

What do you call a really tall, green person who lives on a stalk?

A human bean!

Did you hear about my garden this year?

It was the stalk of the town!

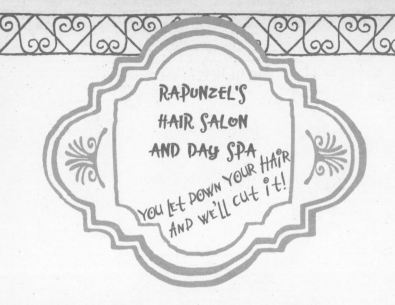

RAPUNZEL'S HAIR SALON AND DAY SPA

YOU LET DOWN YOUR HAIR AND WE'LL CUT IT!

What do you call a princess with a Mohawk?

Ra-punk-zel!

Why did Rapunzel tell her pet rabbit to stretch?

She likes long hare!

What did the farmer say when the rabbits ate all his carrots?

I'm having a bad hare day!

Where does Rapunzel like to shop?

On the mane drag.

Did you hear about the princess who has hair that's fifteen feet long?

I don't know if it's true — it's just hair-say.

Where should Rapunzel go to college?

Hairvard!

Why was the man arrested for stepping on Rapunzel's hair?

Because he was tress-passing!

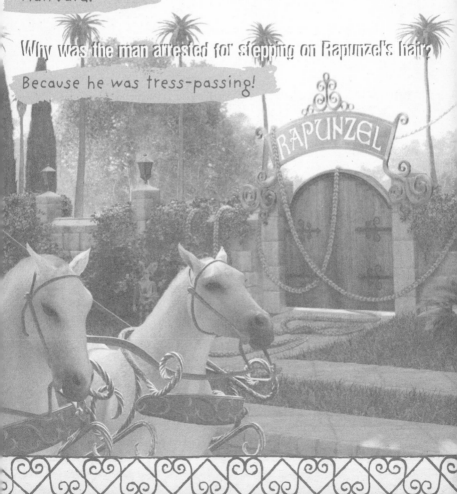

Once upon a time, Little Red Riding Hood was skipping through the forest when she saw the Big Bad Wolf crouched down behind a log.

"My, what big eyes you have, Mr. Wolf," she said.

The wolf looked shocked. He jumped up and ran away.

A little farther into the woods, Red saw the wolf again. This time he was crouched behind a tree stump.

"My, what big ears you have, Mr. Wolf," she said.

Once again, the wolf couldn't have looked more surprised. He jumped up and ran away.

In the middle of the forest, Little Red Riding Hood saw the wolf yet again. This time he was crouched down behind a pile of old rocks.

"My, what big teeth you have, Mr. Wolf," she said. And that's when the Big Bad Wolf jumped up and stamped his feet.

"Will you get lost?" he screamed. "I'm trying to use the bathroom!"

What would you call Little Red Riding Hood if ...

... she was related to Pinocchio?

Little Red Riding Wood.

... her hat kept falling off?

Little Red Sliding Hood.

... she stopped talking?

Little Said Riding Hood.

... she wouldn't stop telling jokes?

Riddle Red Riding Hood.

THE WOLF DEFENSE FUND
IT'S NOT ALWAYS US.

Big Bad Wolf: What do you get when you cross the Three Little Pigs with the Three Blind Mice?

Little Red Riding Hood: I don't know.

Big Bad Wolf: I don't know, either, but I'd sure like to meet 'em!

What's the first thing the wolf ate after he had his teeth cleaned?

The dentist!

WOLF!

Once upon a time, there was a farm surrounded by hills. A little boy lived there — it was his job to mind the animals. If he saw a wolf, he'd cry "wolf" to warn the townspeople of the danger.

In the hills around the farm lived a lonely wolf. Every night, the wolf would howl for hours and hours at the moon.

One day, the little boy got bored. He cried "wolf" one too many times, and his neighbors didn't come to help him when he really did need help. So he ended up being eaten by the wolf. The farm was closed and the animals moved elsewhere.

Suddenly, the night was silent. The wolf stopped howling at the moon.

One night, a bear happened upon the wolf.

"Aren't you the wolf who used to howl all night at the moon?" he asked.

The wolf nodded.

"Well, tell me," the bear said, "why don't you bay at the moon anymore?"

The wolf shrugged and then replied, "No farm, no howl."

WE'VE BEEN KIDDING SINCE THE DAY WE WERE BORN!!

What was the mama goat's favorite TV show?

The Nanny.

How many billy goats does it take to change a lightbulb?

None. They get their kids to do it!

What do you call our facial hair?

Goatees!

Who's our favorite painter?

Vincent van Goat!

Feeling Grumpy? Bashful? Sleepy? Dopey? We can help.

What do you get when you invite Sleeping Beauty and Snow White to your house?

A slumber party that lasts a hundred years!

Why was Snow White chosen to be a judge?

Because she was the fairest in the land.

If Dwarves Had Superpowers . . .

DWARF	SPECIAL POWER
Sleepy	Can seal sleepy eyes together with eye crust in thirty seconds flat.
Dopey	Becomes dumber than a slug in a flash.
Grumpy	Insta-snap allows him to yell at people before they do anything.
Happy	Capable of happiness in any situation. Can smile while eating fish eyes and other ogre favorites.
Doc	Can turn a tissue into a dripping, slimy skin moistener with the snap of a finger . . . or the sneeze of a nose.
Bashful	Supersonic shyness can actually make him disappear.
Sneezy	High-powered snot expressor allows sneezes to blanket entire region.

How does Robin Hood send messages in the forest?

By moss code.

Who brings a basket of food to her grandmother and then steals her jewelry?

Little Red Robin Hood.

Why do Robin Hood's men bend at the waist after they shoot an arrow?

They have orders to hunt with a bow.

How do sheep keep warm in the winter?

Central bleating.

What do you call a sheep on a trampoline?

A woolly jumper!

Hear ye again! Hear ye again!

As it turneth out, every fairy creature in the forest is hysterically funny!

Let it be known that there is no one winner of the gag contest. Instead, EVERYONE is a winner and everyone is invited to the swamp to dine on unidentifiable and often grotesque food.

As one skeleton said to the other, "Bone appetit!"